SUCHOMIMUS

GUANLONG

GIGANTORAPTOR

THERAZINOSAURUS

ERYTHROSUCHUS

OLOROTITAN

LEXOVISAURUS

DIMORPHODON

JOBARIA

EINIOSAURUS

JANE YOLEN

How Do Dinosaurs Say

Merry Christmas?

Illustrated by

MARK TEAGUE

THE BLUE SKY PRESS
An Imprint of Scholastic Inc. · New York

All over the world, people celebrate Christmas in many different ways. We're guessing
no two families celebrate the holiday exactly the same! So how *do* dinosaurs say
Merry Christmas? With an abundance of love, joy, memory, and gratitude.
—J.Y. & M.T.

THE BLUE SKY PRESS

Text copyright © 2012 by Jane Yolen • Illustrations copyright © 2012 by Mark Teague

Library of Congress card catalog number: 2012006171
ISBN 978-0-545-41678-8
10 9 8 7 6 5 4 3 2 1   12 13 14 15 16
Printed in China   38
First printing, September 2012
Designed by Kathleen Westray

To Team Stemple

J. Y.

To the White Family

M. T.

On Christmas Eve,
does a dinosaur sleep?
Does he go
up to bed

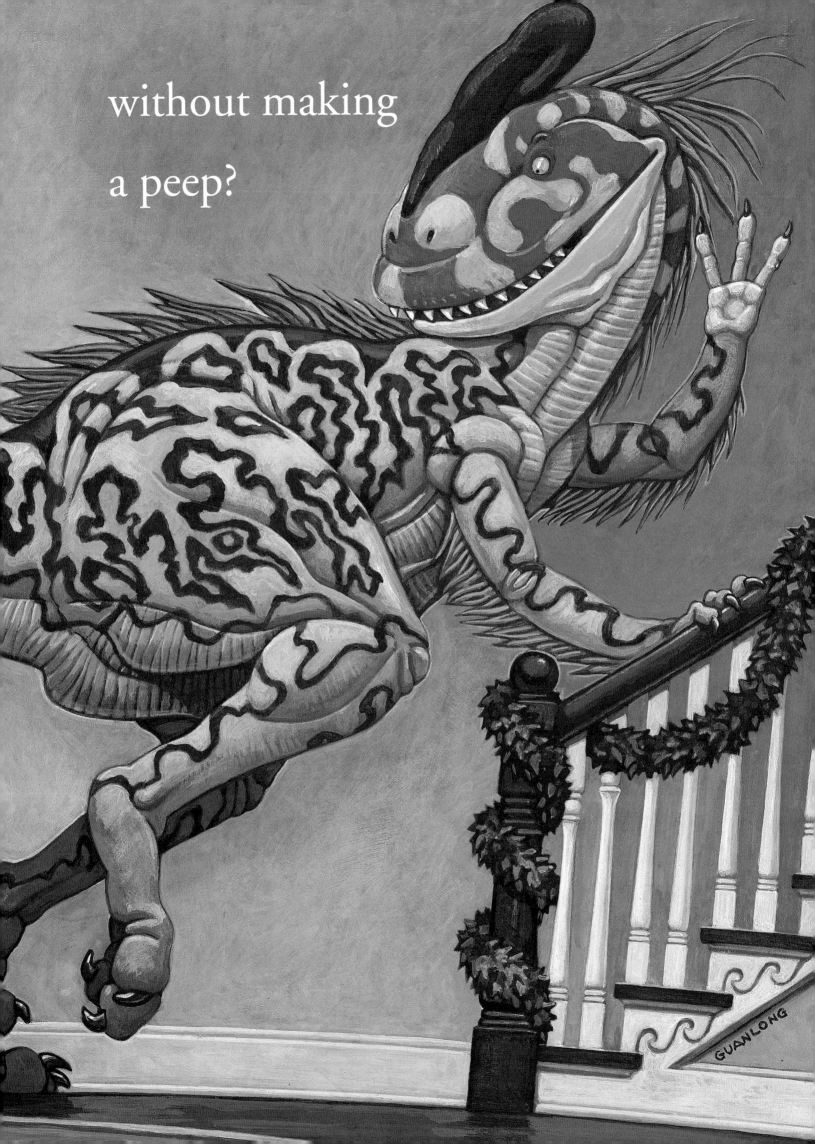

Or does he sneak out,
just to check what's to see?

Does he rip open presents set under the tree?

Does he pick off
some ornaments,
angels and
all?

Does he shake
up the tree
so the rest
of them
fall?

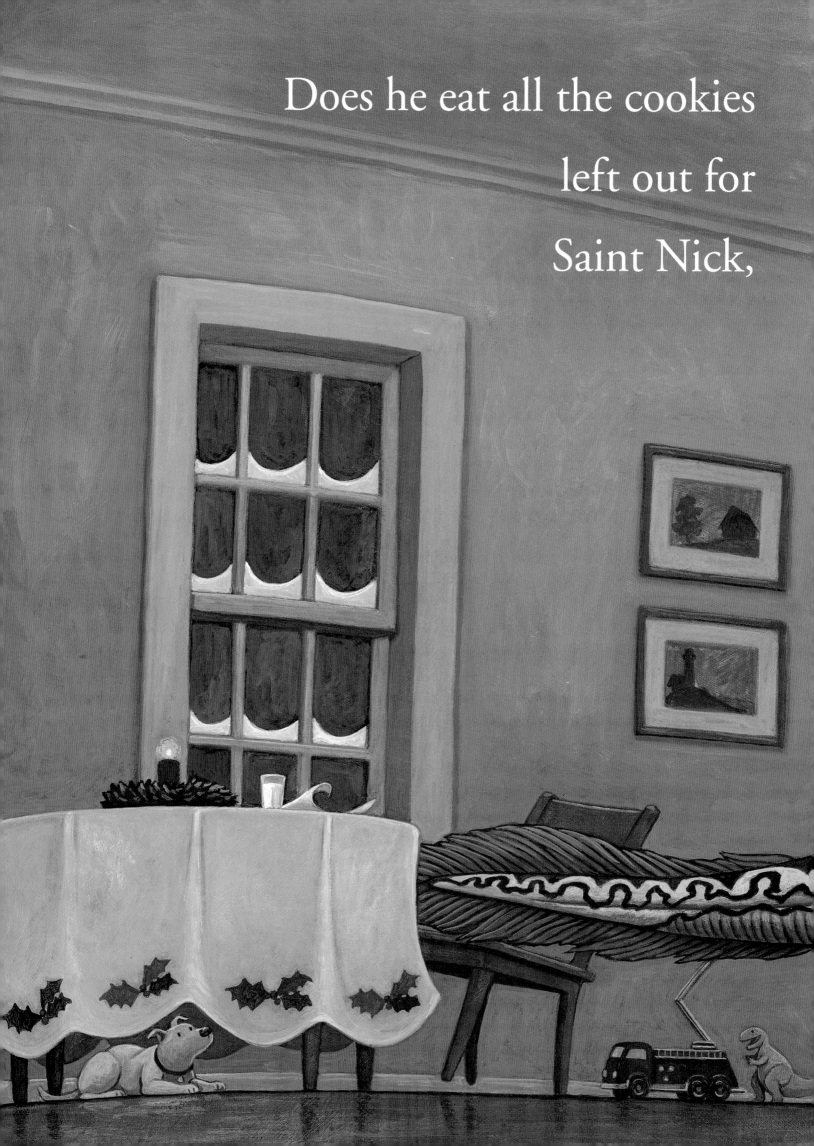

Does he eat all the cookies left out for Saint Nick,

giving each candy cane

one sloppy lick?

Does he up-end

the stockings right

onto the floor?

DIMORPHODON

Does he pick out the best gifts

so he will have

more?

No . . . a dinosaur doesn't.
He carols with care.

He helps trim the tree

so no branches

are bare.

He eats all his dinner,
then clears away dishes,

and gives his grandparents big Christmas Eve wishes.

When Santa arrives,
he's tucked in.
Hear him snore.

Merry Christmas, Merry Christmas, you good dinosaur!

SUCHOMIMUS

GUANLONG

GIGANTORAPTOR

THERAZINOSAURUS

ERYTHROSUCHUS

OLOROTITAN

LEXOVISAURUS

DIMORPHODON

JOBARIA

EINIOSAURUS